When Grandma's Asleep

First published 2019
ISBN: 9781709573941

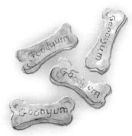

AWARDS

Sophie and William
Joseph and Jessica

Inspirational Cuteness Award

Clever Clogs Award

Brian, Jenny, Sue, Sarah,
Caroline and the Tooth Fairy

Grandma PopPop Gran Grandad Grandpop Mamgu Tadcu

Nan Pappi Bambi Popples Pebbles Dabadoo Snuggy

Pop Twinkles Pawpee Puddy Grandpa Granny Huggy

Hugs and Kisses
Sun and Fun
Shoes and Socks
Fish and Chips
Song and Dance
Rock 'n' Roll
Night and Day
Gin and Tonic
Pencil and Paper
Food and Water
Grandparents and Grandchildren

ONE WITHOUT
THE OTHER
IS NOT
COMPLETE

Lolly Pops Gramms Grampers Nanna Gummy Gumpabear

When Grandma's Asleep

SSSSssshh!
You'll wake her up!
Ouch!
I can't see anything!
You stepped on my toe!
SSshhhh!

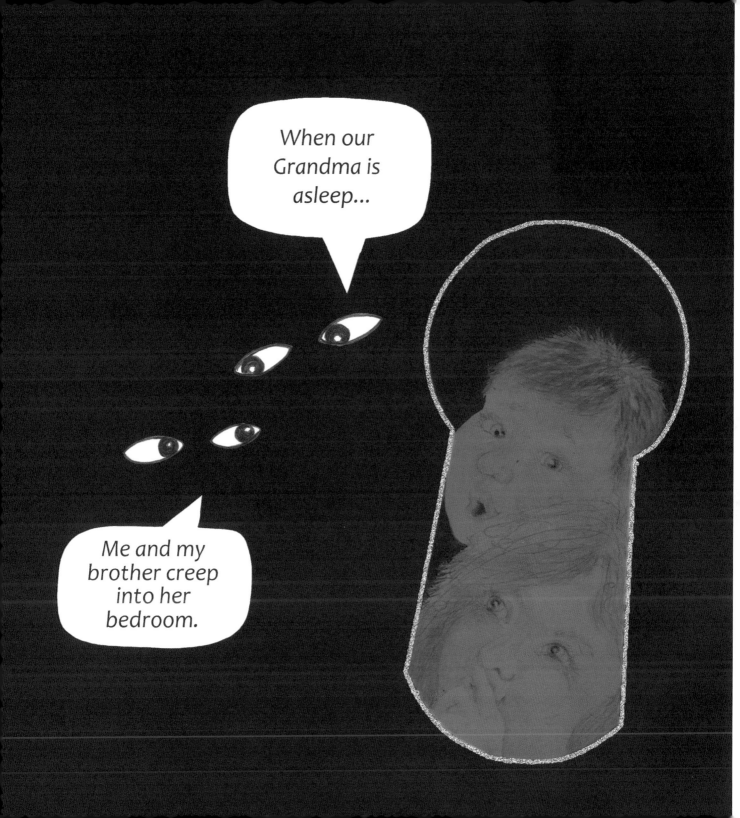

We tiptoe very quietly over to her bed.

And place a red curly wig upon her head.

When she is snoring,
We do some drawing, of a rather fetching moustache,
The kind your Great Uncle George may sport,
With curly up bits as an afterthought.

The Snot Mop

The Pencil

The Soup Strainer

The Toothbrush

The don't be silly

The Handlebar

The Nice Try

The Lampshade

The Frothy Coffee

The Spider

Abracadabra

The Caterpillar

The Cats Whiskers

It *Tickles* and she begins to stir,
And therefore we **DASH** out
FAST and close the door.

We sit on the stair and begin to giggle.

Then dance

and laugh and start to

PIDDLE

oops!

Whats that noise?
It's coming from the attic.
Is it a mouse doing an

RUN!

She's stirring.
The cat's jumped
on the bed and is purring.

We hope it doesn't
wake her up
(or we'll be in trouble).

Hightail it out of here
QUICK on the double!

What's that?
it's smelly!

The cat's been dislodged
from her rotund belly.

It's Grandma!

She's

BLOWN

off

and me and my brother
are starting to cough.

Goggly eyes are a huge surprise. As they **bounce** and **PING** from their socket.

We gingerly place them on her nose,

then

ZOOM

out the room

like a Rocket.

A CLAP of THUNDER

No it's her snoring!
Let's grab some more things,
before it's morning.

Next some lipstick,
the RED kind.

We try to trace carefully around her lip line

but it's terribly difficult
when you're only nine.
(actually I'm five but that didn't rhyme).

Oh cripes! The dog's barking!

We go down and give them a treat,

and they fall back on their beds, fast asleep.

SSSSHHHH

Yogi

now Ella's starting.

Grandma begins to severely cough.

OH NO!

All her disguises nearly

BLEW OFF

Next we need some earings,
(the dangly kind)

with lots of

SPARKLES

and
Crystals
aligned.

I've got some purple ones Aunt Charlotte gave me.
She said they're all the rage in up market Torquay.

Keep
low
I
think
she
saw
us

Flatten
yourself
upon the floor
And stealthily slide
outside the door

Last a hat to ^{TOP} it all.

A **battered** straw boater from Cousin Paul,
(by all accounts he's a real oddball).

Our glorious masterpiece
is at an end.
It is a marvel,
a transformation,
a wonderful

blend

The dressing up box

is empty of disguises.

QUICK! make haste,

before Grandma arises.

Grandma wakes and rubs her *goggly* eyes...

The cat meows and hisses with SURPRISE.

"What's got into him for goodness sake? All I've done is become awake."

Grandma rises

and looks in the mirror

enthralling...

"I look particularly *Beautiful* this morning."

Also in this series
When Grandpop's Asleep

Use these blank pages to create your own disguises…

Printed in Great Britain
by Amazon